THE GREAT PET PANIC

Katie Davies

Illustrated by Hannah Shaw

SIMON AND SCHUSTER

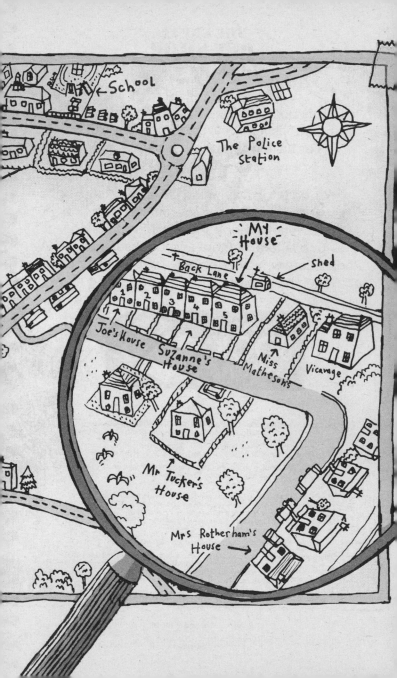

THE GREAT PET-SHOP PANIC

This book has been specially written
and published for World Book Day 2011.
For further information please see
www.worldbookday.com

World Book Day in the UK and Ireland
is made possible by generous sponsorship
from National Book Tokens, participating
publishers, authors and booksellers.
Booksellers who accept the £1 World Book Day
Token bear the full cost of redeeming it.

NATIONAL
BOOK
tokens

This World Book Day book published in Great Britain in 2011 by
Simon and Schuster UK Ltd/Penguin Books

Text copyright © 2011 Katie Davies
Cover and interior illustrations copyright © 2011 Hannah Shaw

The right of Katie Davies and Hannah Shaw to be identified as the author
and illustrator of this work respectively has been asserted by them
in accordance with sections 77 and 78 of
the Copyright, Design and Patents Act, 1988.

Simon & Schuster UK Ltd
1st Floor, 222 Gray's Inn Road, London WC1X 8HB

A CIP catalogue record for this book is available from the British Library.

978-0-95662-765-0

Printed and bound in the UK

www.simonandschuster.co.uk
www.katiedaviesbooks.com

❝ CHAPTER 1 ❞
Pet Theft

This is a story about me, and Tom, and my friend Suzanne Barry, and the time we decided to steal some pets from the pet shop. Tom is my brother. He's five. He's four years younger than I am. I'm nine. I've got another brother, and a sister too, but they're not in this story because they're older than me and Tom, and they don't really care about pets or pet shops or anything like that.

Suzanne lives in the house next door to us. It was her idea

to steal the pets in the first place. Afterwards, when it went wrong, Suzanne said that stealing the pets wasn't her idea at all.

She said, 'I never said *steal*, Anna,' (That's my name.) 'that was *you*. All *I* said was, "what about a *heist*?"'

But I looked 'heist' up in my dictionary, and it said:

heist [high-st] ◆ *noun*
a crime in which valuable things are taken illegally and often violently from a place or person
◆ *verb* to take unlawfully, to *steal*

2

Suzanne wouldn't look at the dictionary, because she said, 'I know *exactly* what a heist is because I'm nearly *ten*, and I've seen *'The Top Hundred Heists Of All Time'* on telly, and my cousin's been in *court*.'

So I started to read what the dictionary said out loud. And then Suzanne put her hands over her ears, and said she couldn't hear. So I said how it didn't make any difference if Suzanne's cousin *had* been in court, because it's not like he was on trial for a heist, because he was only on the school trip, and his whole class went, and I didn't know why Suzanne kept going on about it. And then me and Suzanne fell out. And Suzanne went home to her house. And I went back to mine.

Afterwards, when it got dark, I knocked three

3

times on Suzanne's bedroom wall, and she knocked back three times on mine, which is the code we have. And then we both went over to our windows, and opened them, and crawled out, and sat on our window ledges and talked about things out there, like whether anyone else in the road was still awake, and how far away the stars are, and how if Mum had got us a pet when the pet shop first opened, like me and Tom had asked, we would never have had to plan a heist in the first place.

👣 CHAPTER 2 👣
The Wool Shop

Before the pet shop opened, it used to be a wool shop. And then, whenever Nanna came to stay, me and Tom and Nanna always went to the wool shop together. Nanna loves wool. She says, 'The wonderful thing about wool is it's cool in summer, and warm in winter.'

Which isn't really true because whenever Mum makes me and Tom wear our jumpers, which Nanna knitted, in the summer, we boil and the wool itches and sticks to our skin. And that's why, when Mum tries to make Tom wear his,

he holds his arms down by his sides, and digs his chin into his chest, so she can't get it on him, and has what Nanna always calls The Screaming Habdabs.

Nanna wears wool all year round. She wears a wool hat, a wool scarf, wool gloves, wool jumpers, a wool skirt, wool tights, and a wool coat. The only things Nanna wears that aren't made of wool are probably her pants. I know Nanna's pants aren't wool because me and Suzanne once looked inside them, at the label, when they were hanging on the line. And the label said: '85% nylon, 15% elastane, 100%

cotton reinforced double gusset.'

And then it said, 'superpowered, high-waisted shape suit hosiery with tummy-taming panels, controlling compression zones, and unique rear-end uplift.'

Nanna's pants are much bigger than other people's. And they've got a bra bit attached on top. If you didn't already know they were pants when you saw them, you would probably think they were a wetsuit, or a superhero costume, or something like that. Whenever Mum hangs Nanna's pants out, me and Suzanne always get The Hysterics. And then Mum gets cross and tells us to stop. But the thing with The Hysterics is, once you've got them, you *can't* stop. Especially not the time Mum hung Tom's pants up next to Nanna's. Because Tom's pants are

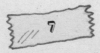

7

tiny. And they made Nanna's pants look even more massive. And that was when Suzanne had The Hysterics so bad she was sick on her shoes.

Anyway, when me and Tom and Nanna used to go to the wool shop, Nanna let Tom chose the colours, which always took ages, and Nanna and the Wool Shop Woman talked about the patterns, and the size of needles you needed, and how they couldn't knit as quickly as they used to, and all that, and I sat on the seat and waited.

But the last time me and Tom and Nanna went in the wool shop, the Wool Shop Woman pointed to a sign that said: 'Clearance. Up to 80% off. All stock must go.' And she told Nanna

8

that the wool shop was closing down.

Tom asked the Wool Shop Woman, 'Why?' And the Wool Shop Woman said because she wasn't selling enough wool.

And Tom asked, 'Why?' again.

And the Wool Shop Woman said it was because people weren't buying it. And Tom asked, 'Why?' again. Because that's Tom's best question, and once he's started asking it, sometimes he doesn't stop.

And the Wool Shop Woman said it was because all her best customers were too old to get out, and young people these days couldn't be bothered to knit, because they were bone idle, and they didn't know they were born.

9

And Tom was going to ask, 'Why?' another time, so the Wool Shop Woman gave him a biscuit, and he started to eat it.

And I said, 'What shop is going to open here instead?'

And the Wool Shop Woman said, 'A pet shop.'

I got up from my seat, and Tom stopped eating his biscuit, and we asked the Wool Shop Woman lots of questions about the pet shop, like when it was coming, and what it was going to be called, and what animals it would have and all that. Because me and Tom like pets a lot more than we like wool. And we had been wanting a pet for ages, ever since our Old Cat died, when it got run over by Miss Matheson in the back lane

The Wool Shop Woman didn't know all that much about the pet shop, except for when it was opening, so after a while Nanna said, 'Come on, Duck, that's enough questions.' And she bought her wool, about a million balls, because she said she wouldn't get angora at that price again. And she told the Wool Shop Woman she would be sorry when the wool shop was gone.

And me and Tom said we would be too.

Even though, like we told Nanna afterwards, a pet shop would be much better.

CHAPTER 3
The Pet Shop

The day the pet shop opened, me and Tom and Suzanne got up early and went and sat on the pavement opposite, and waited. The sign on the front of the shop said: 'The Ark, Purveyor of Fine and Exotic Pets and Pet Paraphernalia.' And there was a picture of Noah, and his ark, and all the animals going inside.

This is what it says 'paraphernalia' is in my dictionary:

Paraphernalia [par-uh-fer-nail-ee-uh] ✦ *noun* equipment, apparatus, or furnishing used in or necessary for a particular activity: *a fisherman's paraphernalia*

After a while, a light came on in the window, and the sign on the door was turned round to say 'Open'.

Me and Tom and Suzanne crossed the road, and opened the door, and went inside.

A bell rang when we walked in. There was a man sitting at a desk at the front of the shop.

'Hello,' Tom said.

'Mmm,' said the man.

'We've come to see the pets.'

The Pet Shop Man didn't say anything.

Tom told him how we were only going to *look* at the pets, because Mum said we definitely weren't allowed any new ones, and if we came back asking, we wouldn't be allowed back to the pet shop again.

The Pet Shop Man didn't say anything. He was reading a magazine. At the top of the page, it said, 'Breeding Rare Pets: How to maximise your profits.'

Tom started telling the Pet Shop Man all about how we used to have a cat, until it got run over by Miss

Matheson in the back lane, and was squashed flat. And he said how Miss Matheson never admitted that she did it. But how we knew it was her, because Suzanne found cat blood on Miss Matheson's car tyres.

The Pet Shop Man said, 'Humph' and turned his page. And I took Tom's hand, because I didn't think the Pet Shop Man wanted to talk anymore. And we started looking around the shop.

It was very different from when it used to be the wool shop. All the shelves which had the balls of wool on were gone, and where they had been, around the walls, were tanks and cages and boxes and crates, stacked up high, all with different animals in. And, in the

15

middle of the shop, there
were two more rows, which made
three aisles. There were different sections
for each kind of animal, a rabbit section with
rabbits of all different kinds and sizes. Giant
Grey Chinchillas, and white Dwarf ones called
Hotots, with big black eyes, and an orange
spotted one with
long floppy ears
called a Holland
Lop. And there was
a bird section with

three white Sulphur-Crested Cockatoos, and
a bright blue bird called a Tropical Lorikeet,
and a massive red parrot
called a Scarlet Macaw. And
there was a small mammals

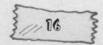

section, with about a million different things

in: Speckled Long-haired Guinea-pigs, and Dumbo-eared Rats, and European Black Bear Hamsters and all that. And there was a reptile

section with a Horn-nosed Chameleon, and a million different tiny bright-coloured Tree Frogs with webbed feet, and bulging red eyes. And there were black slimy Salamanders with yellow spots, and last, there was a spider section, which only had one thing in it, in a small glass tank, and the sign next to it said,

'Mexican Red-Kneed Tarantula.'

'Look!' said Tom, and he reached out to touch the tank.

The Pet Shop Man looked up from his magazine, 'You look with your *eyes...*' he said.

Tom pulled his hand back and stood still, staring at the tarantula in its tank. Me and Suzanne stared as well. But not from as close-up as Tom. Tom's nose was touching the glass.

I'm not scared of spiders or anything like that, because I'm nine, but this spider was the size of about a million normal ones, and it was covered in thick black hairs, and you could

18

see every one of its eight eyes, and there was a cricket in the corner of the tank, which was alive, and the tarantula was walking towards it.

'Shall we look at some of the other pets?' I said.

But Tom wanted to stay looking at the spider because he said he had never seen one like *that* before.

'Aren't you scared of it?' Suzanne said.

'No,' Tom said. 'It's slow, and soft. I want to stroke it.' And he pressed his face even closer to the tank, and his breath made the glass go all misty.

Me and Suzanne went and looked all round the rest of the shop again, at all the different animals. We went round it three times,

19

and each time we came to the end, Tom was still there, where we'd left him, staring at the tarantula.

The Pet Shop Man had stopped reading his magazine. He stood up and came out from behind his desk. 'Where are your parents?' he said.

And I told him how Mum was at home matching up all the odd socks, and trying to get Dad to mow the grass, and how Dad was watching football and all that.

And the Pet Shop Man said, 'Well, you should bring them with you next time. Time to leave now, I'm closing for lunch.'

CLOSED

And he held the door open. So we said, 'Goodbye.' And the Pet Shop Man shut the door behind us and turned the sign to say, 'Closed.'

We went home and told Mum all about all the different pets, and I said how I liked the Black Bear Hamsters best, and Suzanne said how she liked the Lop-eared Rabbit. And Tom said how he liked the Tarantula.

And Mum made a face, and said we shouldn't go getting any ideas because we were not getting a pet. And certainly not a tarantula.

And we told her how the Pet Shop Man said we should bring her and Dad down to the shop to see the pets for themselves.

And Mum said, 'Did he, now?'

21

And she said how she didn't have time to go pottering about in pet shops.

Anyway, after that, me and Tom and Suzanne went in the pet shop all the time, whenever we could. As soon as it opened on a Saturday, and every day after school. And there were always lots of other children in there too. And everyone at school said how it was even better than a zoo because you could go on your own and you didn't have to pay to get in and it had Rare Pets like you didn't see anywhere else.

On Sundays, when the pet shop was closed, me and Tom and Suzanne went in the shed and talked about all the different animals, and which ones we liked best, and made lists, and drew pictures. And Tom did the tarantula every time. And he stuck pictures of it up all over the shed. And Suzanne said that Tom was 'obsessed', because every time we went to the pet shop, the tarantula was all Tom cared about. Sometimes it was hiding in the corner of the tank, and sometimes it was frozen still in the middle, and sometimes it was up on the side, and you could see underneath it.

This is what it says 'obsess' means in my dictionary:

Obsess [ob-sess] ◆ *verb*
to dominate or preoccupy the thoughts, feelings, or desires of (a person); beset, trouble, or haunt persistently or abnormally

One night I had a dream about the tarantula. I was lying down and I couldn't move and the tarantula was walking up my neck towards my face. And after that, every time we went in the pet shop, I tried not to look at the tarantula at all.

Even though the pet shop was much better than the wool shop, the Pet Shop Man wasn't as nice as the Wool Shop Woman was. Because, the wool shop let you look at wool for as long as  you like, and you could touch it, as long as your hands weren't sticky, and she always gave Tom a biscuit, and she didn't mind if you didn't buy anything. But the Pet Shop Man wasn't like that. He never let you touch anything, even if your hands were clean. And when Tom asked him if he had any biscuits, he just laughed. Even though, like Tom said, 'it's not funny.'

And he wouldn't answer any questions about the pets, because he said, 'I haven't got time to stand around talking to kids all day.' Even though, like Suzanne said, he *did* stand around all day anyway, and it wouldn't take any more time up if he talked.

Then, one day, when we got to the shop, there was a sign on the door that said, **NO UNACCOMPANIED CHILDREN**.

So me and Tom and Suzanne went back home and we asked Mum to come down to the pet shop with us.

And at first Mum said, 'No.'

And Tom asked 'Why?' about a million times, and promised he would eat his onions, and stop asking for so many biscuits, and I said I would do my homework, and Suzanne said, '*Please*', and in the end Mum said, 'Alright, alright, but I am *not* going to buy you a pet. We are only going to *look*.'

The Pet Shop Man was much nicer when Mum was with us. He said, 'Hello' when we went in, and asked Mum if she wanted any help. And he showed us around, and asked Mum what she was interested in. Mum said we were just looking. And he asked if we wanted to see some puppies called Neopolitan Mastiffs that he had out the back, which he had never said anything about before, and we said that we did. And he told us all about

the kind of breed that they were. And they were only two weeks old, and they were all in a big cardboard box, sleeping on top of each another. And

they made tiny snuffling sounds.

And, even though we had said that we wouldn't ask for anything, it was hard not to when we saw them.

I said, '*Please* let's get one, Mum.'

And for a second I thought Mum was going to say 'yes.' Because she had her head on one side, and she was biting her lip, and she said, 'Ah, *look* at them . . .' But then she shook herself and said how she already had to look after four children, and Dad, and she wasn't looking after a puppy as well. And she started to walk

£600

away. And then she turned round and looked at them again. And then she said to the Pet Shop Man, 'How much are they, out of interest?'

And the Pet Shop Man said that they were £600. And Mum said, 'Ha.' And then she said, 'Definitely not.' And she went back into the shop, and we followed after. Then the Pet Shop Man started trying to tell her about some of the other pets, like the rabbits, and the lizards, and the tree frogs, which he said were 'less expensive and lower maintenance.'

And then Mum looked out the window and said, 'Looks like rain; the washing's out.' And she walked out of the shop.

On the way up it started raining hard, and I asked again about getting a puppy, and Mum started walking really fast, and saying how you shouldn't really get puppies from pet shops anyway, because you don't know the breeder, or how they have been treated. And how if we *were* going to get a puppy, we didn't want one that had been overbred, we just

wanted a mongrel. And how she didn't know why we were even talking about it, because we weren't getting a puppy anyway.

And then the rain *really* started coming down. And we had to run.

And I said, 'What about a rabbit, then, or an iguana, or a stick insect?'

And Mum said '*No!*' and ran on ahead because, even though she's old and all that, Mum can run fast when she has to, like when she doesn't want to talk about pets, and she wants to get the washing in.

And me and Tom and Suzanne went and sat in the shed. And listened to the rain on the roof.

✋ CHAPTER 4 👈
The Pet Plan

Me and Suzanne and Tom decided we would put all our money together and buy a pet ourselves. And we would keep it in the shed. And not tell anyone. Because we had all sorts of other things in the shed that no one knew about, which we weren't really allowed, like the wasp trap, and the worms, and the homemade stink bombs, and no one ever went in the shed, except Dad to get the lawnmower, when Mum made him, which wasn't very often, because it's hard to make Dad do things.

We made a list of the pets we liked best in the pet shop, and their prices:

Anna's and Suzanne's and Tom's Top Ten List Of Pets

1. Neapolitan Mastiff Puppies £600
2. Lop-eared Rabbit £45
3. Black Bear Hamsters £22
4. Giant Grey Chinchilla £80
5. Hairless Norway Rat £3
6. Horn-nosed Chameleon £72
7. Green Costa Rican Tree Frog £35
8. Stick Insect £13
9. Speckled Long-haired Guinea-pig £17
10. Mexican Red-kneed Tarantula £200

And we went to get all our money together to see what we could afford. Suzanne went to her house, and me and Tom went to ours. I looked in my money box. There was 79 pence, and an old penny that Nanna gave me for luck, and two paper clips. I always spend my money as soon as I get it because, like Nanna says, otherwise it burns a hole in my pocket.

Suzanne came back and said that she only had a pound, which her Mum gave her, and she had nothing else because she asked her Dad for her pocket money and he said she wasn't getting any this week because of not eating her aubergines and losing her left shoe, and all that. Suzanne's

Dad always takes money off her pocket money whenever she does anything wrong. And that's why Suzanne hasn't had any pocket money in ages, and why Mum says me and Tom have to share out all our sweets with her.

When we looked inside Tom's money box there was no money at all. Instead there were lots of scraps of paper that said 'I Owe You…' on them. And they were all in Dad's handwriting. And they said how much money he had taken, each time, and why. We took the I Owe Yous into the shed and Suzanne wrote a sum because I'm not very good at maths, and I always

I owe you £2 - parking

I owe you £15 - pub.

get things in the wrong columns. This is what the sum looked like:

£15.00 (pub)
£04.50 (parking)
£10.00 (bet with Mum about grass cutting)
£07.00 (payment to Andy for mowing lawn
         - that's my older brother)
£36.50 (total)

And then me and Suzanne got pretty excited because that was enough money to buy all *sorts* of pets, like a tree frog, or a hamster, or two prickly stick insects. But Tom wasn't excited because he liked the tarantula best and he wanted to buy that. But the tarantula was £200. Suzanne told Tom how he could have a hamster, four hairless Norway Rats and one stick insect and still have two pounds fifty left over for sweets.

So, in the end, Tom said, 'Okay.'

And we went to find Dad. Dad was watching the football on telly. Tom showed Dad the bits of paper.

And Dad said, 'Ah. Those are as good as money. Those are I Owe Yous. It's all accounted for.'

Tom said, 'Can I spend them?'

Dad said, 'Not exactly.'

I told Dad that Tom needed his money back.

Dad said, 'I haven't got it on me now.'

And I said, 'I'll ask Mum for it.'

And Dad said, 'No, don't do that.'

Because he would get in trouble for taking the money from Tom's money box.

'I'll go to the bank,' he said.

Me and Tom and Suzanne waited.

'What, *now*?' Dad said.

I said, 'Yes.'

Me and Tom and Suzanne walked down with Dad to the cashpoint, and he got the money out, and he gave it to Tom.

Dad said, 'What's it for, anyway?'

And Tom told Dad how he was going to buy four rats, a hamster and a stick insect. And Dad said, 'Oh.'

Then we went to the shed. And me and Tom and Suzanne counted the money out. And then there was a knock on the door.

'What's the password?' I said.

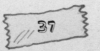

And Mum said, 'Four rats, a hamster and a stick insect.'

And then she said how she wanted Tom's money, and she would look after it for him, and he wasn't allowed to buy pets with it.

I didn't say anything.

After a while, Mum said, '*Anna*,' like she always does, 'hand it over.'

I poked the money through the spy hole in the shed. And then all we were left with was my money and Suzanne's, so we added that up and there was £1.79. Which meant we couldn't afford anything. Except some ants. And they weren't really the kind of pet that we wanted. Because, like Tom said, we can get them for free from under the shed.

And that was when Suzanne said, 'What about a heist?'

CHAPTER 5
Pet Shop Panic

First we made a list of all the things we would need.

Anna's and Tom's and Suzanne's List Of Things We Need To Do A Heist

1. Binoculars
2. Three balaclavas (ask Nanna to knit them)
3. Three pairs of gloves (so no fingerprints)
— Nanna to knit them
4. One sack (to put the pets in)

Nanna was pretty pleased that we asked her to knit us balaclavas. Because normally she can't find anyone who wants her knitting them anything, so she started straight away.

Suzanne showed me and Tom how we should walk to stay hidden: flat against the walls, and doing short fast runs and stepping side to side, like crabs. And how to drop to the floor if something happened. And she had a special sign for ducking down, which was when she touched the top of her head. And we practiced it over and over again. And Tom had his burglar costume from his birthday, which had a stripy top and an eye mask and a bag that said SWAG on it. Which Suzanne said she didn't think was very good because it gave it away, so Tom turned the swag bag inside out so no one would know. And we practiced all week, after school, and when it came to Saturday, we were ready. Except for the balaclavas which Nanna was bringing.

I stood looking out of the bedroom window waiting for Nanna to arrive. When she came up the path I ran down to meet her.

'Have you got the balaclavas?'

Nanna said that she did and she gave me a brown paper bag.

I said, 'thanks' and I ran back in the house and knocked on the wall three times for

41

Suzanne to come and meet me at the shed, and then I went and got Tom.

I passed Suzanne the brown paper bag. She opened it.

'What are *these?*' Suzanne said.

The balaclavas Nanna had knitted were pink and orange and red and all sorts of colours and they were made of fluffy mohair, not plain black like Suzanne had said. But we put them on anyway because Tom liked his, and it was too late to get Nanna to make any more, and, like I told Suzanne, they still hid our faces. So we put them on.

When we got down near the pet shop we looked through the binoculars. And we waited until someone else went into the shop, like we had planned, so we wouldn't set the bell on the door off. And while the customer was talking to the Pet Shop Man we got down on our hands and knees and crawled in through the door. And we lay flat on the floor and slid closer to the cages. It was quite hard to see through the mohair around the eyes of the balaclavas. I was just about to open the tank of the tree frogs, when I heard the bell on the door ring, and saw Suzanne run out of the shop. I saw a man's shoes and they were very shiny, and he had on some smart navy blue trousers, and a blue jacket with silver buttons, and on his head was a policeman's helmet. I stayed very still. The policeman got out his badge, and he showed it to the man at the front desk, and he started pointing around the shop. And then I panicked. I wondered who had told the policeman, because it was only me and Tom and Suzanne who knew about the heist, unless someone had snuck into the shed and seen the plans. I tried to get Tom, but he was sitting in front of the tank, staring at the tarantula. If I ran out of the shop without him, Tom would be trapped, but if I went round to get him, the policeman would see me. I decided to create a diversion. On the shelf above my head was the box of live crickets that the Pet Shop

44

man used to feed the tarantula. I took off the lid, and gave it a shake. One hopped out, and then another one, and another one,  and another, and they started hopping and jumping all over the shop. And the tarantula ran to the front of the tank, and the rabbits started twitching and thumping their back legs on the floor of their cages, and the rats scratched at their bars, and squeaked, and the parrots went, 'Caw, caw, caw.' And the Pet Shop Man started running around trying to catch the crickets, and the policeman started running around trying to catch the Pet Shop Man. And I grabbed Tom, and ran out of the shop.

☙ CHAPTER 6 ☙
The Spider Heist

When we got back to
the shed, Suzanne was
already there. Tom
was holding the top of
his bag very tight, and
he was shaking. And we
shut the shed door behind

us. And we turned off the light, and blocked
up the spy hole so it was all dark. And I said
how Suzanne shouldn't have run off, and how
she was supposed to be the lookout and all
that. And how we could never go out again
because the policeman would be looking for

us. And Suzanne said how it would be alright because of the balaclavas, and how we should probably burn them or bury them because if anyone saw them they would know it was us. And I said how the heist had been rubbish because we didn't even get an ant. And Tom was standing very still, holding his bag tight.

Tom said, 'I got something.'

'What?' I asked.

And Tom said, 'A *spider.*'

I gulped. There was only one spider for sale in the pet shop. The tarantula.

Tom put his swag bag on the table and took the tie off the top of it. He slowly opened the bag up.

And me and Suzanne stood back, and said, **'No, Tom, don't!'**

47

But Tom tipped the bag upside down anyway.

I looked away at the wall, and Suzanne shone her torch on the table, and I saw the shadow of the spider on the wall of the shed, and I screamed.

And then I heard Suzanne laugh, and I looked at the table and there, in the middle of it, was quite a small, ordinary spider. And Tom said how it was on the floor, in the corner, and it had just walked straight into his bag. And how he had heisted it from the shop. And he put the spider in a jam jar, with a dead fly, and some twigs.

And me and Suzanne laughed.

But Tom didn't because he said it wasn't funny.

And we said how we thought he had the tarantula, and Tom said how this was a tarantula baby.

Tom watched the spider every day, and cleaned out its jam jar, and waited for it to grow into a tarantula.

The next time we went to the pet shop, it was shut, and Nanna said she had seen the Wool Shop Woman who had told her that the pet shop had been closed down while the police investigated where the Pet Shop Man had got his rare frogs and parrots from and a very poisonous kind of Mexican Red-Kneed tarantula, which was an endangered species.

Me and Suzanne looked up 'endangered'

in the dictionary, and this is what it said:

Endangered [en-dane-jer-d] ✦ *adjective*
At risk, especially of becoming extinct

And then we looked up 'extinct'.

Extinct [ex-tink-t] ✦ *adjective*
Having no living members (of a species)

And Tom said how the tarantula wasn't endangered *or* extinct because he had its baby in a jam jar and his friend had told him that spiders have lots of babies so soon there

would be lots of Red-Kneed tarantulas in our shed and maybe we could give some back to Mexico.

Suzanne and me just smiled. And we never told Tom that it was just an ordinary spider, like the ones we sometimes get in the bath.

And that was the end of the Great Pet-Shop Panic.

SURPRISING SPIDER FACTS!

1. Tarantulas shoot or flick spiky hairs from their abdomens at their enemies when threatened.

2. Some people in South America eat tarantulas — apparently they taste like peanut butter!

3. Tarantulas aren't that poisonous to humans — a bite is like being stung by a hornet or a bee.

4. Some tarantulas can live for 25 years.

5. Funnel Web spiders in Australia can hold their breath for up to 72 hours straight.

6. Larger spiders can catch bats, birds, fish and even snakes in their webs.

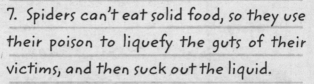

7. Spiders can't eat solid food, so they use their poison to liquefy the guts of their victims, and then suck out the liquid.

8. The smallest spider in the world is called Patu Marplesi, and you could fit ten of them on the end of a pencil.

9. Spiders have 48 knees each! (six joints each for eight legs)

10. Spider silk is the toughest material known on earth; it's so strong that if you made a web big enough, it could stop a Boeing 747 jet in the air.

11. Little Miss Muffet was a real girl — she was the daughter of Dr Muffet, who made her eat spiders as he believed they had healing powers when eaten.

12. Fear of spiders is called 'arachnaphobia' [uh-rack-nuh-fo-be-ah]

Katie Davies

Katie Davies was born in Newcastle on Tyne in 1978. In 1989, after a relentless begging campaign, she was given two Russian Dwarf hamsters by her Mum for Christmas. She is yet to recover from what happened to those hamsters. THE GREAT HAMSTER MASSACRE is Katie's first novel. It won the Waterstones Book Prize in 2010. She also wrote THE GREAT RABBIT RESCUE and THE GREAT CAT CONSPIRACY. Katie lives in North London with her husband, the comedian, Alan Davies, and their baby daughter. She does not have any hamsters.

Hannah Shaw

Hannah Shaw was born into a large family of sprout-munching vegetarians. She spent her formative years trying to be good at everything; from roller-skating to gymnastics, but she soon realised there wasn't much chance of her becoming a gold medal-winning gymnast, so she resigned herself to writing stories and drawing pictures instead!

Hannah currently lives in a little cottage in the Cotswolds, with her husband Ben the blacksmith and her rescue dog Ren. She finds her over-active imagination fuels new ideas but unfortunately keeps her awake at night!

THE GREAT HAMSTER MASSACRE

Katie Davies

THE GREAT HAMSTER MASSACRE

WINNER
Waterstone's
Children's Book
Prize 2010

"Funtastic!"
MICHAEL MORPURGO

"10 out of 10"
LOUISE RENNISON

Can Anna, Tom and Suzanne discover who is behind the hamster homicide?

THE GREAT
RABBIT
Rescue

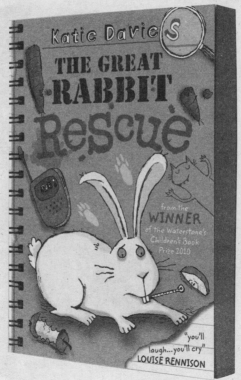

Will Joe-down-the-road
and his New Rabbit be
reunited in time?

THE GREAT CAT Conspiracy

Who is behind the disappearance of the New Cat? It's time for another investigation...

If you enjoyed THE GREAT PET-SHOP PANIC
look out for the next book about Anna,
Suzanne, Tom and Joe-down-the-road...
Here's an extract from
THE GREAT CAT CONSPIRACY,
coming soon!

The Fish Head

The night before it went missing, the New Cat caught a fish in the Vicarage pond. Not a small fish like Joe-down-the-road once won at the school summer fete. Or a middle-sized fish like Mum gets on Friday from the chip shop. This was a Really Big Fish. It was the biggest thing the New Cat has ever brought in. And it must have taken ages to catch it, and kill it, and drag it down the road, and get it in through the cat flap.

In the morning there were bits of fish all over the house. There was a tail on the kitchen table, and scales all up the stairs, and a backbone on the bathmat and, on Tom's pillow, when he woke up, was a big fish head with its eyes wide open.

I wouldn't like it if the New Cat put a fish head in *my* bed, but Tom didn't mind. He shouted out, 'Hey, Anna, come and see *this*.'

So I went into Tom's room. And he sat up in bed. And he pointed at his pillow.

'It's a fish head,' I said.

Tom said, 'Do you think it's a present from the New Cat?'

And I said I thought it probably was. Because I didn't think anyone else would give a present like that.

'The New Cat likes me *best*,' Tom said. And he got out of bed, and he picked up the fish head, and he took it into Mum's room, where she was still asleep, and said, '*Look!*' And he held it near Mum's face.

Mum opened her eyes, and said, '*What the…? Tom*, it's a *fish head*!'

And Tom said, 'Yes.'

'Where did you *get* it?'

'In my bed.'

'Give me *strength*,' Mum said. And she looked at her clock, and then she shot out of bed, because she had overslept. And she grabbed the fish head off Tom, and ran downstairs, and she got the tail off the kitchen table, and she put them both in the bin. And then she ran back up, and brushed her teeth, and picked the bones up off the bath mat, and hoovered the trail of scales all up the stairs.

And she said, 'I'm going to Church...' Because it was Sunday. 'If anyone's interested? *Stinking* of *fish*.'

Mum didn't used to go to Church much because she only went sometimes to keep Nanna company. But, after Nanna died, when  it was her funeral, Mrs Constantine asked Mum if she could put her name down on the handing out the hymn book rota. And Mum meant to say 'no', but she said 'yes', by mistake. And after that she had to go to church all the time. Because the other people who hand out the hymn books were always going away on holiday, and getting glandular fever, and things like that.

When Mum goes to church, me and Tom go

to Sunday School, next door, and do painting, and putting on plays instead, and Tom eats all the biscuits.

Dad doesn't go to Church. He doesn't even believe in God. He says he believes in staying in bed.

After Church was over, and the Vicar had finished standing by the door, and shaking everyone's hands, and saying, 'Go in peace and serve the Lord', he came back inside where Mum was putting the hymn books away, and I was waiting, and Tom was collecting up all the cushions for kneeling, and putting them in a big pile by the pulpit (which is the thing the Vicar stands on to speak). And the Vicar said, 'Hello', and, 'lovely day', and 'put the cushions back now, please.' And then he asked

Tom what we had done in Sunday School.

Tom said how we had eaten biscuits.

And the Vicar said, 'Anything *else*?'

And Tom shook his head . . .

The Vicar didn't look very pleased. And he breathed in deep, and he did a sigh. And then he did a sniff. And he said, 'Can anyone else *smell fish*?'

Mum stopped putting the hymn books away.

And the Vicar said, 'I've got fish on the brain. Several of mine have gone missing from my pond. There was another one gone this morning when I got up - my best Koi Carp.'

Mum didn't say anything. But Tom did. He said, 'Mum smells of fish.'

And the Vicar said, 'I'm sure she doesn't.'

And Tom said, 'She does, because the New Cat brought a big fish in through the cat flap and it killed it and put its bits all over the house. And Mum had to clean it up. Its head was on my pillow.'

And the Vicar said, 'Oh? What did this fish *look* like?'

And Tom said, 'Like *this*.'

And he held his eyes wide apart and rolled them around and stuck his tongue out.

And the Vicar said, 'What colour was it?'

And Tom told the Vicar how it was hard to tell what colour it was because it was in lots of different bits because its scales were all up the stair and its tail was on the table, and its bones were on the bathmat. And some of it was missing, but its head, which was in his bed, was white and orange with black spots.

And the Vicar said, 'That's my best *Koi Carp*! I bought him for breeding…'

And Tom said, 'He's in the bin.' And then he said, 'Are there any more biscuits?'

And the Vicar said, '*No*. There *aren't*.' And his neck went all red.

WIN!

Are you desperate for a pet all of your own? Did your parents say NO when you asked?

Fear not, because you could WIN the coolest, cheekiest toy pet around:

DAVE THE FUNKY SHOULDER MONKEY!

Dave is simply irresistible. He's charming and adorable, he's cute and mischievous. Fix him to your shoulder, position the remote control in your pocket and interact with him as though he was a real monkey. Amaze and amuse your friends and family!

To enter a competition to win DAVE and a signed set of all Katie Davies' hilarious animal books go to www.katiedaviesbooks.com and answer a simple question – good luck!

Finished
this story?

DON'T
PANIC!

Flip the book over
for another
great read...

PUFFIN BOOKS

Reading . . . it's for wimps, right?

I mean, what's the point? All it does is improve your spelling and get you to use your imagination and stuff. And maybe find out facts and help your vocabulary. And entertain you. But, other than that, it's just useless.

OK, so it helps you get clever so you can pass a few exams. But what's the point of exams anyway? I mean, apart from helping you get a better job. And earn a bit more money. And be happier and more successful.

Reading. For wimps? Or for winners? Your choice!

Andrew Cope believes reading is one of the most important life skills you will ever learn. He reads at least four books a week. Andrew is currently teaching his pet dog, Lara, to read. She really likes this book! You can find out more about the Spy Dog and Spy Pups books online at www.spydog451.co.uk, where there are pictures, videos and competitions too!

Books by Andrew Cope

Spy Dog
Spy Dog 2
Spy Dog Unleashed!
Spy Dog Superbrain
Spy Dog Rocket Rider
Spy Dog Secret Santa
Spy Dog Teacher's Pet
Spy Dog's Got Talent (for World Book Day)

Spy Pups Treasure Quest
Spy Pups Prison Break
Spy Pups Circus Act
Spy Pups Danger Island

SPY DOG'S GOT T★LENT

ANDREW COPE

Illustrated by James de la Rue

PUFFIN

To all the World Book Day readers — keep up the good work!

PUFFIN BOOKS

Published by the Penguin Group
Penguin Books Ltd, 80 Strand, London WC2R 0RL, England
Penguin Group (USA) Inc., 375 Hudson Street, New York, New York 10014, USA
Penguin Group (Canada), 90 Eglinton Avenue East, Suite 700, Toronto, Ontario, Canada M4P 2Y3
(a division of Pearson Penguin Canada Inc.)
Penguin Ireland, 25 St Stephen's Green, Dublin 2, Ireland (a division of Penguin Books Ltd)
Penguin Group (Australia), 250 Camberwell Road, Camberwell, Victoria 3124, Australia
(a division of Pearson Australia Group Pty Ltd)
Penguin Books India Pvt Ltd, 11 Community Centre, Panchsheel Park, New Delhi – 110 017, India
Penguin Group (NZ), 67 Apollo Drive, Rosedale, Auckland 0632, New Zealand
(a division of Pearson New Zealand Ltd)
Penguin Books (South Africa) (Pty) Ltd, 24 Sturdee Avenue, Rosebank, Johannesburg 2196, South Africa

Penguin Books Ltd, Registered Offices: 80 Strand, London WC2R 0RL, England

puffinbooks.com

First published 2011
001 – 10 9 8 7 6 5 4 3 2 1

Text copyright © Andrew Cope, 2011
Illustrations copyright © James de la Rue, 2008, 2010, 2011
All rights reserved

The moral right of the author and illustrator has been asserted

Set in Bembo Book MT Std 15/18 pt
Typeset by Palimpsest Book Production Limited, Falkirk, Stirlingshire
Made and printed in Great Britain by Clays Ltd, St Ives plc

British Library Cataloguing in Publication Data
A CIP catalogue record for this book is available from the British Library

ISBN: 978-0-956-62765-0

www.greenpenguin.co.uk

Penguin Books is committed to a sustainable future
for our business, our readers and our planet.
The book in your hands is made from paper
certified by the Forest Stewardship Council.

1. A Sheepish Dog

'Brilliant, Ma,' yapped Star. 'You did it. You *actually* did it!'

Lara looked at her young pup, a little embarrassed. All she really wanted was to be a normal family pet and here she was, through to the final of *Have You Got Talent?*

'It's especially brilliant,' perked up Ollie, 'because one of the judges hates animal acts.'

Lara nodded. She was torn between feeling proud that she was the most talented dog on the planet and feeling sheepish that she was performing her comedy dog routine in front of millions of viewers. *It's not quite what I was trained for*, she thought. Lara cast her mind back to her days as an MI5 spy dog.

She had been trained by Professor Cortex,

1

Britain's top animal scientist. *If anyone's got talent, it's the prof*, thought Lara. *I started life as GM451, a highly trained secret agent. But one of my missions went pear-shaped*, she remembered, putting a paw to her bullet-holed ear. *So now I'm a family pet, and there's no better family than the Cooks. But I've still got plenty of talent*, she smiled, counting on her paws. *I can defuse bombs*, she thought. *And drive a car. And send emails and understand English, French, Chinese and even basic Cat. I've been on dangerous missions around the world and caught more baddies than most people have had hot dinners.* Lara had run out of paws. *And now here I am, trained to juggle, break-dance and play the guitar!*

She looked around at the Cook children's beaming faces. *They don't seem to mind me being on the telly*, thought the retired spy dog.

Ben wore a permanent grin. Lara was officially the whole family's pet but, as the eldest child, Ben was the pack leader. He and Lara had bonded from the start, spending their days playing football or fishing at the river. Ben even had a framed photo on his bedside table of Lara holding her first trout.

Lara turned to Sophie, who was dancing around the living room with excitement. She was so proud of her talented dog and was very excited to see behind the scenes of a TV show.

The youngest Cook child, Ollie, was just being Ollie. He was a good talker. And getting his pet dog voted through to the final of *Have You Got Talent?* gave him plenty to talk about!

'I thought it was pretty cool when you did the spinning-on-your-head thing,' he beamed. 'But you should have seen the judges' faces when you played the guitar!'

'And now you've got to come up with something even better,' grinned Sophie. 'Remember what the lady judge said? She really liked you but you needed to do something special for the final.'

'And then she cried!' gasped Ben.

She always cries, thought Lara. The family pet looked at her two puppies, Spud and Star, wagging as if their lives depended on it.

'Do you get any food you want in your dressing room?' yapped Spud.

'We can come, can't we, Ma?' pleaded Star. That gave Lara an idea. *The final is in two weeks' time*, she thought. *I wonder if we could get you guys involved too . . .*

2. Cool Collars

The next two weeks were solid practice. It was Professor Cortex who'd dared Lara to go on *Have You Got Talent?* 'Your spy-dog days are long gone,' he'd said. 'So it doesn't really matter who knows about your talents now.' He'd persuaded Lara that, after hiding her brilliance for so many years, it was time to come out. 'Show the world what a top dog can really do,' he'd challenged. 'It's time to shine, GM451. The West End beckons. Or movies. Or a pop career . . .'

Calm down, old fella, thought Lara, cutting him short with a bark and a wave of her paws. *I draw the line at singing! Have you heard me in the shower? It's definitely howling rather than singing!*

Lara had decided that she wanted to get her puppies involved in the final. She figured that they'd get extra votes for their cuteness. So the three of them practised, along with the professor.

The prof couldn't help himself and had issued the puppies with special collars.

'They light up,' smiled the professor, 'so you'll look like stars. But they've also got gadgets built in as usual.' The dogs had concentrated hard while the professor explained. 'Yours, Star, has a built-in button . . . here.' He showed the puppy, frowning through his spectacles. 'It releases a small dart, like so.' The professor aimed at a chair and clicked. The children couldn't see anything but they heard a tiny click as the dart embedded itself in the chair. 'Poison,' smiled the professor. 'Well, laxative actually.'

'What's "laxative"?' asked Ollie.

'It makes you, you know,' said Sophie. 'Go to the loo. Really quickly.'

Ollie grinned. 'Cool,' he said. 'Emergency toilet situation. Can I try it on my teacher?'

Professor Cortex frowned. 'Most certainly

not, young man,' he barked. 'This is not a practical joke. It's a serious gadget for eliminating baddies.' The professor's tone changed, sounding calmer. 'And your collar, Agent Spud, has this button here.' He peered through the glasses that had slipped down his nose and pointed. 'It opens a pouch containing glue.'

'Glue?' snorted Sophie. 'That's not very special. I think you'll find glue's already been invented.'

'Not any old glue,' huffed the professor. 'You've heard of superglue? Well, this is *ultra*glue. Sticks anything. And I mean *anything*. Forever. And I mean *forever*!' He looked down at Spud, who was wagging at one end and panting with excitement at the other. 'Be very careful, young puppy,' warned the professor. 'Anything. Forever,' he reminded.

Spud's tongue lolloped out of the side of his mouth. He loved his food. His immediate thought was to glue himself to the fridge. *Food . . . forever*, he dreamt, licking his chops.

3. Weirdos

It was the night before the final. The Cook family stayed in a cheap bed and breakfast while Professor Cortex and the dogs were put up in a fancy London hotel. They were invited to have dinner with the other finalists. Lara eyed the competition, weighing up the dogs' chances of winning.

There was a young singer from the North whose mum was very poorly. *Sympathy vote*, thought Lara. There was a husband-and-wife sword-swallowing act. *Gruesome vote*. Sitting at one side of the table was a troupe of dancers from Scotland. *All dressed in tartan. Everyone north of the border will vote for them!* Then a fat man who dressed as a woman he called Gloria, and sang very badly. *The worst cabaret act ever,*

8

remembered Lara. Next to him was a pair of break-dancers from London. *'Hip' and 'Hop'? Too corny.* A singing grandma from Wales. *Grandparent vote. Howls a bit like me.* And, last but not least, sitting on her left, a ventriloquist from Manchester who appeared to make his puppet talk. *The dummy's good*, remembered Lara, *but he's pretty hopeless. A real outsider.*

The weird group all sat at the table, awaiting their starters, talking excitedly about the next day's final. Lara looked around and savoured the moment. The professor looked happy, chatting away to the break-dancers and enjoying his champagne. The puppies had cleared the crisps and Spud was helping the Scottish dancers with their peanuts. The ventriloquist wasn't smiling much. *Perhaps he's just shy*, guessed Lara. *Or nervous. It's going to be a big day tomorrow!*

All of a sudden, the national anthem started up and the double doors swung open. *Wow, who's this?* thought Spud, looking up from the bowl of peanuts he'd been hoovering up. A waiter entered the room and announced, very rigidly, 'Please be upstanding for tonight's guests of honour.'

Spud had a peanut stuck up his left nostril. 'Cool,' he snorted, sending the peanut pinging into a champagne glass on the other side of the room. 'It must be the Queen!'

The performers fell silent as they stood. All eyes went towards the door. In walked the *Have You Got Talent?* judges, doing the royal wave as they moved towards their seats. The contestants clapped enthusiastically, except Spud, who started chomping on a bowl of olives.

The judges sat down and that was the cue for the performers to sit. Lara and the professor found themselves next to the judge who was the most difficult to please. He droned on and on about how awful some of the earlier rounds had been. And how difficult it was to be a judge. And what a curse it was to be right all the time. And about how he didn't think a dog act could ever win *Have You Got Talent?*

The professor nodded politely, but Lara was determined to prove him wrong.

4. *The Fame Game*

Finally it was the big day. The contestants were ferried to a London theatre in a fleet of limos. Lara and the pups sank into the comfy leather seats, swishing the blackened windows up and down and playing with the gadgets. Star was imagining what it must be like to be truly famous. The professor looked a little uncomfortable.

'Twenty million viewers tonight,' he reminded the dogs, mopping his brow with a hanky.

'Cool,' yapped Spud. 'The whole country will be tuning in to see the most talented dog family in canine history!'

'Maybe we'll be a hit on YouTube too,' said Star excitedly.

11

The car queued for a few minutes while the other competitors got out of their limos. Star stood on her hind legs and peered out of the car window. She could hear screams and see flashes going off as the competitors made their way into the theatre. She wagged extra hard. *The final of* Have You Got Talent?, *the biggest TV event of the year, and we're finally here!*

Eventually it was their turn. The limo pulled up at the front of the theatre. Cameras flashed. Mobile phones were waved in the air as the professor emerged from the car. He shielded his eyes from the flashbulbs. Several microphones were pushed into the scientist's face.

'How do you see it going, old man?' asked one reporter, without giving him a chance to answer.

'How do you feel about one of the judges hating dog acts?' yelled another.

But the biggest cheer was reserved for the dogs. Spud fell out first, shades on, waving to the crowd. Star was next, a bit shyer than her brother, managing a gentle wave of her left paw.

Lara was last out. She stood on her hind legs and stretched to her full height, almost as tall as the professor. She fixed her shades in place, put her arm round the scientist's shoulder and did her best doggy grin. *This one's for the front page of tomorrow's papers*, she thought as she performed for the cameras. *We'll show that dogs have talent.*

The professor and his 'Dynamic Dogs' act disappeared into the theatre, the door closing on the din.

'Phew!' gasped the professor. 'That's a wild crowd!'

The group was led to what the production manager called the 'green room', even though it was white. The professor was served lots of drinks and encouraged to relax before he went on live TV. Star wasn't good at sitting still so she decided that she and her brother should explore. 'Let's go and find the judges,' she wagged. 'Maybe we can get autographs!'

Spud wasn't so keen on getting autographs but he figured they might come across some sausage rolls on their travels. 'Can we, Ma?' he asked.

Lara was practising for her performance, and warming up for her singing. She stopped howling to answer. 'Just don't be too long. We'll have to get ready soon. And don't get lost!'

The puppies nosed their way along a few corridors, going deeper and deeper into the theatre. They could hear that the auditorium was filling up fast. They peeked in at a few doors. The dressing rooms were getting busy. The kitchen staff were hurrying to the judges' rooms, bringing caviar and champagne. There was a production and editing room, which was full of people and TV screens. Star explained that this was where the show was put together. *Sophie would love to see this*, she thought.

Spud wandered to the far end of the corridor and sniffed at the final door. He looked up at the sign. *No entry*, it read. *Strictly forbidden*.

No sausage rolls in there, he thought. As Spud turned to leave, he heard a noise from inside the room. He raised his bullet-holed ear and listened. *There it is again*, he thought. *I wonder what's in that room that's so top secret?* The spy

puppy cocked his head and listened carefully. All was quiet. He was just about to give up when there was another noise, this time overhead. He looked up at the ceiling. *Someone, or something, is shuffling along in the air vent*, he thought, looking up at the narrow metal tube above his head. *Must be a very small person*. He followed the tube to its end. *Yikes, a rope ladder!*

'Sis,' he woofed, 'come and check this out.'

Star bounded to the end of the hallway and both pups stood outside the top-secret room. 'The prof told me this is where the voters' phone calls end up,' said Star, wagging her tail hard. 'You know, when people phone in for their favourite act? It's all done electronically. Only takes a few seconds. Your call is registered on a computer server . . . in there,' she said. 'And a pound is automatically transferred from the caller and banked.' Star stopped and thought for a second. 'I wonder how many votes there will be tonight,' she yapped excitedly. 'It's a very important room. That's why nobody is allowed in. Ever!'

Spud's eyes widened. 'But somebody *was* in,' he woofed quietly. 'And now they're out.

In the air vent. Up there,' he whined, jabbing a paw towards the ceiling.

As Spud pointed, a white ceiling tile was removed and a head poked down. The face peered around, failing to see two small puppies standing in the shadows. Thinking the coast was clear the small figure eased itself on to the rope ladder and hung for a while, making sure the tile was fixed back in place. Now he was in the light the pups could see it was just a boy. Then he swung down the rope ladder before unhooking it and tucking it into a rucksack.

Star and Spud looked at each other and blinked. 'Are you seeing what I'm seeing? I know that boy from somewhere,' whined Star. 'Why is he creeping about in the roof space? And what on earth was he doing in the computer room?'

The boy padded silently down the carpeted corridor. Spud looked at his sister and took a deep breath. 'I think we may have stumbled across another adventure!'

5. Eyes Down

The Cook family took their places in the audience. 'Remember,' said Dad, handing out *We ♥ Lara* banners, 'hold these up and cheer as loudly as you can. The Professor and Dynamic Dogs are on second.'

'Who's on first?' asked Ollie.

Dad consulted the programme. 'The ventriloquist,' noted Dad. 'Funny man with that weird talking puppet, remember?'

Ollie shuddered. 'I don't like him. He's spooky. In fact, he's not funny at all, just scary.'

At that moment the audience erupted as the judges walked on to the stage and took their seats, the men on either side of the glamorous lady. The theme music started up and the crowd went wild. Ben, Sophie and

Ollie waved their banners and yelled at the tops of their voices. The two presenters came on and whipped the audience into even more of a frenzy, reminding them that this was indeed the final and that a magnificent prize awaited the winners.

'A slot on *The Royal Variety Performance*!' they shouted. 'And who wouldn't want to win that?' All the competitors crowded on to the stage and waved. Star and Spud jumped about excitedly and posed for the TV cameras before they cut to the first advert break. Mum, Dad and the children settled into their seats, waiting for the show to start again.

After more music and joking from the presenters, the first act was introduced. Darren Smith was certainly an odd-looking man. He had a very old-fashioned comb-over hairstyle, with his parting starting just above his right ear. His long saggy face made it difficult to guess how old he was. Most people guessed at about fifty but he was actually a decade younger. And, even though he looked sad almost all the time, here he was on national TV, about to entertain the crowd with his ventriloquist act.

'He doesn't look very entertaining,' whispered Mum.

'I don't know why the judges put him through,' agreed Sophie.

The man sat on a stool in the middle of the stage and the crowd quietened while he got ready. Darren opened a case on the floor in front of him and pulled out a puppet. It was a boy in a school uniform. Cap, shirt, stripy blazer and shorts. He had wobbly arms and legs and a wooden-looking face. The audience shifted uneasily. Ollie was right, it was a bit spooky.

One of the presenters spoke. 'Welcome back, Darren,' he said. 'Congratulations on making it to the final.' He waited a while and smiled as the crowd went wild. Somehow, the word 'final' always brought the house down. 'Remind the viewers, Darren, what is it that you do for a living?'

The man almost raised a smile. 'I work in a bank,' he said quietly.

'Great,' lied the presenter. 'That must be really exciting.'

'Not at all,' replied the man.

'It's what this programme is all about, Darren. People like you getting the chance to entertain millions of people on live television. Now, remind us what your act is,' he said.

'I'm going to entertain you tonight,' he announced, 'with my little friend Woody.' The puppet raised its head and grinned a wooden smile at the audience.

'Excellent,' smiled the presenter as the crowd clapped. 'Darren Smith and, er, Woody . . . take it away!'

The professor was flapping in the dressing room. 'I'm not sure this is such a great idea,' he gabbled, swallowing a handful of his heart tablets. 'I mean it seemed like a great idea at the time — when I dared you to audition, GM451,' he said. 'But now? What if the judges don't like us? You know that you-know-who hates dog acts.'

Lara nuzzled the prof. She sometimes wished she could talk but that was beyond even a spy dog. *It doesn't matter about the judges tonight, Prof*, she thought. *It's the viewers at home who decide. The pups and I have a really cool act*

lined up. Trust us. We won't let you down. All we can do is our best.

Star and Spud were hyper. They couldn't wait to do their act and then get back to the computer room to sniff out an adventure.

'We're on next,' howled Spud. 'I'm sooo excited,' he yelped, chasing his tail round and round until he was dizzy.

Star called her brother over to the TV. 'Check this out, Spud,' she woofed. 'Take a look at Darren and Woody and tell me what you notice.'

Spud stared at the screen. The ventriloquist was in full flow. 'Well, he's absolutely rubbish for a start,' woofed Spud. 'And his comb-over is a disaster.'

'Not Darren, silly. Look at Woody . . . the puppet.'

Spud gazed at the TV. Darren Smith was drinking a glass of water while Woody rabbited on about being at school.

'That's a pretty cool trick,' admitted Spud. 'How does he do that?'

'Look at the dummy, dummy!' woofed his frustrated sister. 'Because it's *not* a dummy.

It's that boy who came down from the rope ladder.'

Spud slapped a paw against his forehead. 'I knew I'd seen him somewhere before,' he woofed. 'What on earth's going on, sis?'

There was no time to think as a lady wearing headphones and carrying a clipboard walked into the room. 'Follow me to the stage, please!'

The professor and his performing dogs were ushered out of the dressing room to take their place in the wings. They stood behind the curtain and caught the end of Darren Smith's act as the judges made their comments.

'I don't know how you do it!' said the judge on the left.

'Mesmerizing!' said the lady judge.

'It was . . . OK,' said the main judge, and the crowd booed and hissed. The Cook family clapped politely.

Then, before they knew it, Lara and the puppies were centre stage.

6. Wooden Acting

The professor was incredibly nervous. The children sat in the audience, fingers crossed, banners at the ready. They'd persuaded the professor that he didn't need his white lab coat and that he should dress casually. The scientist had looked puzzled, as if 'causal' was a foreign word.

Ben held his head in his hands as he looked at the stage and saw the professor in 'casual'. 'Sandals and socks, Prof,' he said, shaking his head. 'It's hardly catwalk stuff.'

The children clapped and cheered as the professor put the dogs through their paces. There where whoops of delight as the puppies juggled balls to and fro. Star was especially good, balancing a ball on her forehead like she'd

seen premiership footballers do in their warm-up. Then, as their finale approached, the crowd went silent and there was a drum roll.

Lara stood on her hind legs, a tall and proud dog. Spud scampered as fast as his stubby legs would carry him and somersaulted on to Lara's shoulders.

'Ta da!' he woofed, his smile wobbling as much as his legs. The audience applauded.

'And now for the big finish,' hissed Sophie, crossing her fingers and screwing her face into a bundle of hope.

Star walked calmly to the side of the stage. She looked at Lara. *She's tall*, thought the tiny puppy. *And with Spud on her shoulders, even taller*. Star had fallen several times in practice. But she thought of the *The Royal Variety Performance*. She imagined the thrill of meeting the Queen. Star looked into the audience and picked out the children. 'Let's do it!' she woofed, sprinting for all she was worth.

The tiny puppy launched herself as high as she could go. Lara bent her knees and the puppy made it, her paws digging into Spud's shoulders. There was a bit of staggering until

eventually Lara straightened her legs and the canine tower stood, strong and firm.

'The world's f-first ever acrobatic canines,' the professor stuttered into the microphone, swishing his hand towards the dogs.

The theatre audience went wild. Three children wilder still. The presenters came on and congratulated the professor and shook paws with Lara and the puppies. 'Over to the judges,' said the good-looking presenter. 'What did you make of that?'

The judge on the left rather liked it. 'It was fun,' he smiled. 'And that's what this show is all about.' The crowd agreed. Sophie waved her banner.

The glamorous lady in the middle wiped a tear from her eye. 'I used to have a dog,' she sniffed, 'and you guys remind me of him so much. You've got talent. Real canine talent.'

It was warm under the theatre lights. The dogs panted as they waited for the main judge to have the final say. Lara and the pups knew he could make or break their chances. He looked stern. 'Everyone knows I don't like animal acts,' he said, 'and you are no

exception.' The crowd booed. The judge turned to face the audience. 'If you'll just let me finish,' he said. 'I genuinely didn't like your act,' he said, pausing for effect and raising an eyebrow to the camera, 'I absolutely *loved* it! You, sir,' he said, pointing at the socked-and-sandalled scientist, 'are in with a genuine chance of winning this show.'

The cheering was still ringing in Lara's ears as the dogs bounded offstage and the presenters cut to the next ad break. The professor and dogs were ushered back to the green room to wait while the other contestants were put through their paces. Star and Spud were delighted their act had gone so well but determined to sniff to the bottom of the mystery as soon as possible.

Darren Smith was sitting in the green room, perched on the edge of his chair, his sad face twitching nervously. Woody's case lay at his feet. Spud sniffed the case but the ventriloquist shooed the puppy away.

'Will you please keep your dogs under control?' he warned the scientist.

Professor Cortex wasn't a people person,

but he knew a miserable face when he saw one. He called Lara and the puppies to his side. The dogs eyed the other finalist suspiciously.

'I need the toilet,' said Darren. 'Probably nerves.'

The ventriloquist stood, grabbed his suitcase and made for the door. Spud quickly woofed an explanation to his mum. 'We don't think "Woody" is a puppet at all. He's a real boy. We think he's been snooping in the computer room,' wagged the puppy excitedly. 'You know, where all the votes come in and the money is sorted. We saw him come down a ladder from the ceiling nearby.'

Lara listened carefully. This could be serious.

'And why's he taking his puppet to the toilet?' wondered Star aloud.

Professor Cortex was sitting comfortably in his chair.

'Let's check it out,' Lara woofed to the puppies. 'Once a spy dog, always a spy dog.'

Lara and the puppies nosed their way out into the hallway. Darren Smith was disappearing through a fire-exit door.

'Come on, guys,' woofed Star, 'he's getting away. Let's nab him.'

As the fastest and fittest, Star was first through the door.

Darren Smith was clattering his way down the fire-escape stairs. Star realized the only way to catch up was to use the banister. The puppy leapt aboard. She crouched low and let go, sliding downwards on her furry tummy. It was a slow start but the puppy gradually gained speed. *Whoa!* she thought as she came to a bend. Star lowered her ears and squinted into the wind as she zoomed round the bend and, before she knew it, she was sailing past Darren Smith. The puppy landed with a crash as the banister ran out. She sat up, head spinning, and recovered her senses. Smith was hurtling down the stairs, taking them three at a time. *I have to stop him,* she thought, *and get to the bottom of this mystery*.

Darren Smith saw the puppy and hesitated. Star raised her hackles and growled her meanest growl. The man stopped in his tracks, dropping his case. Star was only a puppy but she sure had sharp teeth. His case fell open and out tumbled his puppet.

Woody squealed as he hit the floor. 'Watch what you're doing, idiot!' yelled the schoolboy, rubbing the back of his head. 'We're supposed to be escaping. I've fixed the computers so all the money is diverted into our account. Come on, man, it's the perfect crime. Let's scoot!'

Star growled again. The boy got to his feet. 'It's only a puppy,' he said, coming halfway down the last flight of stairs and aiming a kick at Star. The spy pup grabbed the boy's ankle and sank her teeth into the flesh. He yelled and kicked harder, sending Star sprawling.

The boy and man were racing back up the stairs when Star remembered her gadget collar. *Thanks, Prof!* She took aim, pressed the button and fired the poison dart. *Yes!* she thought as it punctured Woody's right buttock. *Direct hit!*

'Ouch!' yelped the boy as he kept climbing the steps. 'What was that?'

'Keep running!' yelled Darren. 'That puppy will come after us!'

Star heard them slam the door on the floor above her, then the sound of her mum and brother coming down the stairs. She met

them on the first floor and quickly explained what had happened. 'They're stealing all the viewers' cash,' she barked. 'Darren Smith and Woody! They're going to make millions!'

'Not if we can help it,' woofed Lara. 'Come on, pups. It seems this really is a spy-dog mission.'

7. Stuck!

The schoolboy was easy to find. Star's dart had done the trick so they knew exactly where he'd be. Spud had sneaked into the toilet on the first floor and waited. Within minutes Woody rushed in, groaning with pain. He had tummy trouble like never before!

The boy slammed the cubicle door shut and managed to pull his shorts halfway down before the explosion.

Spud sat in the cubicle next door, grimacing. *Oh dear*, he thought, listening to the blasts of wind, *that doesn't sound good!* Spud wafted a paw across his face. *And it doesn't smell too great either!*

Eventually the noises stopped. Woody's

moans had become a whimper, but that was just the start of his worries.

Any second now, thought Spud, smiling in anticipation.

There was another cry from the cubicle next door. 'Ouch,' he heard. 'I'm stuck!'

Spud poked his head under the door. *That's my ultraglue*, he smiled. *You're going nowhere. In fact, you're going to be stuck on the toilet for a very long time indeed!* Spud nosed his way out of the Gents. *One baddie caught*, he thought. *One to go.*

Lara and Star had followed Darren Smith back into the theatre. He was panting heavily. He desperately needed an exit but instead he found himself on the side of the stage. He could see the sword swallower and his assistant, their performance in full flow.

Lara approached the man and bared her teeth. Darren had seen what damage the puppy could do and this dog was much bigger.

Lara curled her lip, revealing her white fangs.

'Give up, Smith,' she growled. 'We're voting you off!'

Darren Smith panicked. There was only one way to run and before he thought twice he took it. The audience gasped as the first act reappeared onstage, followed by two of the dogs from the second act. The sword swallower was about to finish. His assistant was handing him the biggest sword he'd ever swallowed. The drum was rolling but the audience was confused. Was this all part of his act?

Darren Smith grabbed the sword from the assistant. The crowd gasped again. Sophie's face disappeared behind her fingers as the evil ventriloquist started swinging the blade round his head. 'Come any closer, doggies, and you'll meet my sharp new friend.'

Lara backed off but the TV cameras zoomed in, capturing every moment. Severed limbs would guarantee worldwide exposure.

Darren Smith's eyes had gone from sad to mad. They darted around, looking for an escape route. There was another gasp as he swung the sword at a rope and the curtain fell,

leaving the dogs one side and him on the other. By the time they'd wriggled through the huge velvet drapes, the ventriloquist was gone.

8. The Dash for Cash

Darren Smith wasn't concerned about anything but the cash. He was happy for the other contestants to have the fame and magazine deals. He'd calculated that there would be twenty million viewers and about half would vote. That was ten million times one pound. The maths was simple – a cool ten million pounds, now being redirected into his bank account. Woody was his thirteen-year-old nephew, a total loser at school but with computer skills to die for. And, calculated Darren, small enough to gain access to the computer room through the air vent.

The plan was hatched. Woody knew computers but Darren worked in a bank. 'We're the ultimate crime team,' he'd assured

his nephew. 'Britain really has got talent. *Criminal* talent! Neither of us will ever need to work again!' Smith had disguised Woody as a dummy. He'd waxed his face and drawn some lines on his mouth like he'd seen on Pinocchio, then added a silly school uniform and the rest was history. Nobody would suspect a puppet. His nephew reprogrammed the mainframe computer and redirected the cash. Then Darren used his job in the bank to hide the accounts, so there was no trail for the police to follow.

The risky bit had been getting to the final so Woody could be in the building to hack the computers on the night. Darren and his nephew had worked hard at perfecting the water-drinking part of the act. Darren drank while Woody chatted; it was bizarre enough to get them to the final.

Now, with the closed curtain causing chaos on live TV, the ventriloquist had opened a trapdoor and jumped through. He found himself beneath the stage in semi-darkness. He walked, head bent, his sword held out to stop him bumping into things. Smith could hear pandemonium above and he knew those

dratted dogs would soon sniff him out. He needed a means of escape. And quickly.

Smith finally made it out from under the stage and found himself in a corridor he recognized. 'The performers' dressing rooms!' He knocked on one of the doors.

'Who is it?' came a voice. It was Gloria, the man who dressed up as a lady for his act. He would be the last to go on tonight.

Darren entered the dressing room. Gloria sat in front of the mirror, applying the last of his make-up, dressed in a sparkly yellow dress. He saw Darren in the mirror and noticed that the sad face of earlier had been replaced by an evil face. And a huge gleaming sword. Gloria's heart and false eyelashes fluttered. He fainted, a line of lipstick across his chin.

Spud caught up with Lara and Star. He explained that Woody was stuck on the toilet.

'Good work, son,' said Lara. 'He won't be going anywhere.'

'Quick, let's follow Darren,' said Star. 'Noses to the ground!'

The dogs sniffed their way to the trapdoor. Spud had the best nose, so he followed the scent from there along a corridor to Gloria's dressing room. 'In there,' he whined. 'The track stops right here.'

Lara stood on her hind legs and pulled the handle. The ex-spy dog was being ultra careful because the man was armed and desperate. Gloria's dressing-room door creaked open.

'Nothing,' woofed Lara as she entered the room, circling on her hind legs, upright in

karate stance. Suddenly there was a banging noise coming from the cupboard. Lara whined, indicating to the puppies to be careful. 'I'll yank the door open and you guys get him.'

Star and Spud nodded, their hackles raised in preparation for attack. Star bared her teeth, ready for a fight. Lara yanked the handle and the cupboard door swung open. But instead of Darren Smith, Gloria fell out. The fat man rolled around on the floor in his vest and knickers, his hands and feet tied and his mouth taped over.

Lara pulled the tape away and Gloria spat out a sock. 'He's escaped,' sobbed the man. 'With my favourite yellow frock!'

9. Catch 22

With the action onstage and the final act nowhere to be seen, the rest of the show was cancelled. The Cook children joined the professor and dogs backstage in their dressing room, promising to meet their parents for dinner in half an hour.

'Tell Professor Cortex I want to know exactly what Lara and Star were doing onstage,' said Mum, giving them a concerned look. 'And that means no more excitement for any of you, do you understand?'

All three children nodded, but they kept their fingers crossed behind their backs.

When they arrived backstage Gloria was sitting in a dressing gown drinking hot tea. He was in shock, gibbering about how Darren

Smith had stolen his dress and locked him in a cupboard.

'So we're looking for a ventriloquist dressed in a bright yellow ball gown,' said the professor.

It's got to be the worst disguise ever. He shouldn't be hard to spot! thought Lara.

'Let's go!' said Spud, bounding out of the door and leading the way.

Sophie and her brothers looked at each other. 'Maybe it won't take long?' she suggested. 'We'll be back in half an hour for dinner, I'm sure.'

'They can't have an adventure without us, can they?' said Ollie, and all three children chased the professor and the three dogs into the hallway.

Ben pressed the bar on the emergency-exit door and the small gang found themselves on the bustling streets of London. 'Which way, GM451?' asked the professor.

Spud put his nose to the pavement and sniffed. 'Mmm,' he wagged, 'hot dogs! With mustard. Someone's dropped one right here,' he woofed, nosing half a sausage off the

pavement.' Lara gave him a glare and his nose returned to the task in hand. 'Thataway,' yelped the spy pup, lolloping towards the River Thames.

Ben was the first to spot the yellow dress as Darren Smith jumped aboard a bus. He saw the dogs and waved, knowing they'd never catch up. And he was right. By the time the children and dogs had sprinted there, the bus was gone. 'That was the number twenty-two,' gasped Professor Cortex, 'heading for Tower Bridge. He'll probably get on the underground there and, if he does, we've no chance of finding him.'

'So let's follow,' urged Ben.

'How exactly?' asked the professor, hands on hips, gasping for breath.

'We can get a taxi,' suggested Ollie. 'But they're all full,' he said, as several whizzed by.

'We can get a bus too,' suggested Sophie.

Lara woofed, her tail wagging at the thought of catching the baddie. She spotted an old London bus parked nearby. 'And if we drive it we can take a short cut,' she barked.

It was a sightseeing bus with an open top. *It's perfect! Come on, gang. All aboard!*

The driver and conductor were busy selling tickets to a long line of customers as the spy dog jumped on to the bus and beckoned the pups. 'Come on, guys,' she woofed. 'We've got a baddie to catch.' Star and Spud leapt after their mum.

'Uh-oh,' said Ben. 'I think Lara has a plan.' The professor and the children raced after the dogs.

'We need you, Prof,' Lara barked, jabbing a paw at the scientist and then the steering wheel. 'For driving duties.'

Professor Cortex looked very unsure. 'GM451,' he began, 'I hope you're not thinking what I think you're thinking?'

And I hope you're not thinking of not *doing what you think I'm thinking*, thought Lara. 'Pups,' she woofed, 'drag him aboard.'

Spud and Star each grabbed a trouser leg and pulled. The professor's socked-and-sandalled feet kicked out but he was helpless. Ben helped pull the scientist aboard and he was plonked in the driver's seat. There was a cap hanging up

and Ollie gave it to the professor. 'Tower Bridge, please, driver,' he grinned.

'Your mother is not going to be happy about this, young man,' said the professor, reaching to turn the key.

As the bus shuddered into life and lurched into the busy road, the real driver chased after it but couldn't catch his bus. He stood in the middle of the street, shaking his fist before reaching for his radio. 'Police,' he shouted, 'I want to report a stolen double-decker, driven by an old man and accompanied by three kids and three dogs.'

10. The Bridge of Sighs

The professor wasn't the best driver. He was OK in a car, but a bus was a different matter. The bus was old and the steering wheel massive. Ben helped him wrestle the vehicle round the corners. The professor slammed on his brakes as they approached a red light.

'No time to stop, Prof,' howled Lara. 'Just go for it. Nobody's going to argue with a double-decker bus.' The dog looked for a gap in the traffic then kicked the professor's foot off the brake. The bus lurched into the junction, car horns blaring and tyres screeching. Black smoke belched out of the exhaust as the ancient engine worked harder than it had ever worked before.

Lara grabbed the professor's iPhone and

logged on to the satnav function. 'Next right,' she woofed, jabbing her paw towards a side street. 'We can get to Tower Bridge before him if we take a short cut.'

Ben and the professor did as Lara suggested, turning the heavy steering wheel sharp right, the bus almost tipping over as it screeched round the corner. They found themselves in a very narrow street with no footpath. It was barely wide enough for a car, never mind a bus. The professor was sweating, but he kept his foot to the floor, the diesel engine rattling angrily. The bus clipped the building on the right, sparks flying. Then it rebounded towards the left wall and there was a loud scrape as more sparks flew.

'Junction ahead,' yelled Ben. 'Give way. Lara, we have to stop. Do we want left or right?'

'Left this time,' indicted Lara as the professor slammed his sandalled foot on the brake and the bus shuddered to a halt. At the back of the bus Ollie, Sophie and the pups held on tight as the bus stopped suddenly.

Outside on the street, Mrs Brady was coming back from visiting her sister in hospital. She

was glad to be healthy. *Apart from my eyesight,* she thought, *I'm in perfect shape for an old lady. Oh good, and here comes my bus.* The bus stopped and she stepped aboard, bus pass open.

Sophie and Ollie looked at each other in horror as an old lady got on to the bus, which started to move again.

Sophie smiled at the lady, doing her best to look like everything was fine. 'Um, hello,' she said. 'Where to?'

'Tower Bridge?' asked the old lady.

'Sit down,' she offered. 'That's, erm, exactly where we're going.'

In the driving seat the professor crunched the bus into gear and hauled the steering wheel left along the Embankment, towards the famous London bridge. He swerved to miss a cyclist and Mrs Brady nearly fell out of her seat.

'Bumpy ride,' smiled Ollie. 'It's because my brother's helping to drive.'

Mrs Brady smiled weakly. 'How long has your brother been a bus driver?' she asked, making polite conversation.

'Oh, he's not a bus driver,' explained Ollie. 'He's still at school.'

'Still at school?' chuckled Mrs Brady. 'How old is your brother?'

'He'll be thirteen in March,' chirped Ollie.

Mrs Brady's smile faded. Her knuckles whitened as she gripped the metal bar tighter.

11. The Leaning Tower

Darren Smith was panting and panicking about his disguise. He'd decided that a man in a bright yellow ball gown was hardly going to be able to blend into London life. *Bad move*, he thought to himself as he sat on his bus, the other passengers eyeing him shiftily. *But at least it means I get a seat to myself.*

Then he heard a police helicopter above. The chopper was beaming live pictures back to Scotland Yard. A crowd of police officers had gathered to watch the footage. Nobody had seen anything quite like it as the pair of double-deckers raced across London. A TV helicopter had joined the scene, with live pictures being beamed across the news networks.

People were peering out of the windows of the bus, looking into the sky, pointing at the helicopter. It was very low and seemed to be following the bus. Smith's heart sank as he heard a voice over the megaphone.

'Bus driver, pull over!' announced the booming voice from above.

Darren knew there was no way that could be allowed to happen. The next tube station was just across Tower Bridge. *If I can get there, I can lose the dress and disappear on the underground network*, he thought. *Ten million pounds richer!*

His decision was made. He struggled to the front of the bus in his yellow gown and pulled the sword from his underwear. He turned to face the passengers. 'Everyone sit down,' he yelled. 'Do as I say and no one will get hurt.'

The passengers screamed in terror. They had never seen such a shiny yellow dress, or had a sword held in their faces by a madman. The driver saw the gleaming metal pointing right at him and decided to do whatever the man in the frock wanted.

'Just drive,' commanded Smith. 'Very fast.'

★

Mr and Mrs Cook had looked everywhere for the kids and dogs when they didn't turn up to meet them. Eventually they'd returned to the green room to see if they'd gone back there. Mum needed a lie down after the stress of seeing Darren Smith threaten the other acts with a sword, and then Lara and Star chasing after him. Dad looked at the TV screen in the corner of the room. There was a red band at the bottom of the picture with the words *Breaking News* flashing across. He stood in front of the TV, eyes widening, and turned the volume up. The shots showed two double-decker buses hurtling along the road, parallel to the River Thames. Dad suddenly had a familiar bad feeling.

Mum was stressed. 'I don't know where the kids have wandered off to,' she huffed, plonking herself in front of the TV. 'I just hope they've not got themselves into another ridiculous scrape.'

The TV news helicopter came alongside the bus and zoomed in. The picture very clearly showed the professor hunched over the steering wheel, Ben helping him drive. Mrs Brady

looked stony-faced. Ollie saw the helicopter and waved at the camera. Spud saluted. Mum fainted.

Desperation had gripped Darren Smith. His comb-over had gone haywire, his bald patch revealed for the world to see. He looked in the bus wing mirror and saw a sightseeing bus weaving through the traffic behind. He looked again, squinting to get a decent look. The professor was driving, a boy squeezed in beside him. 'And I can see dogs!' he cursed. 'Not those blasted dogs from the show! Faster, man,' he instructed the driver, waving his sword. 'They're gaining on us.'

The professor was proud of his old bus. The temperature gauge was rising but his ageing vehicle was gaining on the shiny new one ahead. Oncoming cars were swerving out of the way. Ben was having fun with the horn, blasting out a warning to whoever might be thinking of crossing the road. But even the pavement wasn't safe. The professor had clipped a couple of bins, sending rubbish spilling on to the streets of London. A

lamp post was bent double. A mobile pancake stand had taken a clip too, spraying food all over the pavement. Spud had considered jumping off to help clean up the mess, but the thrill of the ride was too good to miss. He watched the London sights whizz by. *Plus*, he thought, *it's probably not very safe to jump off at this speed!*

Smith's bus was racing ahead. He could see his destination, the most famous bridge in the world, designed to lift up and let ships pass through. And that was exactly what Tower Bridge was starting to do at that moment as a tall sailing ship chugged up the Thames towards it. The barriers had come down to stop traffic driving across the bridge while the road was raised, allowing the mast to squeeze under. Smith looked at the barrier ahead and then back at the ancient bus. Then ahead again. He knew it was dangerous but the risk of losing ten million pounds was greater. He decided to go for it.

'Foot to the floor,' he commanded, thrusting the sharp sword towards the driver.

12. Traffic News

The driver glanced at him, trying to keep his eyes on the road. 'Are you mad?' he yelled above the noise of the screaming engine. 'The barriers are down. The bridge is lifting. We'll never make it!'

Smith prodded the sword at the man's arm, puncturing the skin. A trickle of blood stained his white shirt. No words were needed. 'But I can try,' he blurted, his foot pressing harder on the accelerator. The passengers braced themselves. The upstairs passengers realized what was happening and tumbled down the stairs.

Smith waved his sword one last time. He was the most menacing man in a yellow ball gown anyone had ever seen. 'Sit down,' he

screamed, his hypnotic eyes wild with panic, 'all of you. And hold tight!'

The bus lurched on to the empty side of the road where the oncoming traffic was waiting on the far side of the bridge. It crashed through the barrier, wood splintering, security guards waving their fists.

The bridge controller stopped the bridge opening any further. He looked at the gap and the fifteen-tonne bus. 'Stop!' he shouted, but it was too late as the bus flew up the raised bridge as if it were a ramp, and took off into the air.

The doctor had been called to the dressing rooms. He wafted smelling salts in front of Mum's nose and she woke with a start.

'What?' she began. 'Where?' Who?' She came to her senses and Dad held her hand reassuringly. Mum looked back at the TV screen just in time to see a double-decker bus take off across the gap in Tower Bridge. Her hand went limp and she slumped back in her seat.

★

Nobody was quite sure if the first bus would make it. The professor was a bit odd at times, but not mad. He'd pulled his old bus up at the broken barrier and the children and dogs had tumbled out on to the pavement to watch.

Mrs Brady had thanked the professor for getting her to Tower Bridge so quickly. 'I wish more drivers were as good as you,' she'd said.

The other driver, with a sharp sword pressed against his throat, had given it his best shot. Tower Bridge was opening, but thankfully not even half raised. He'd taken a decent run up the slope and the double-decker had left the ground.

'I've never seen a bus fly,' gasped Ben as it took off.

'Except on *Doctor Who*,' reminded Ollie. 'That was cool.'

But buses can't fly far. The engine whined as the wheels left the tarmac. The double-decker lurched into the air, nose pointing upwards before gravity took hold. The police and TV helicopters hovered, capturing the moment that the bus fell to earth, crashing

across the other side of the gap. The front end had made it across but the back was wedged on the near side. Onlookers waited while the dust settled and the bus smashed on to its side, bridging the gap. There were gasps from the crowd who had gathered to watch.

One of the passengers kicked open the emergency door and a dozen dazed people, including the driver, fell out of the back of the vehicle, tumbling down the slope to safety. The crowd cheered and the emergency services rushed to help them. But one person was missing. All human and dog eyes went to the other side of Tower Bridge. There was no sign of a ventriloquist in a sparkly gown. The helicopters hovered, cameras focusing on the driver's cab. The bus creaked again as it thought about falling through the gap.

Darren Smith had been thrown about but he was OK. He looked down at the grey river below and gulped. He fumbled for the emergency-exit button near his head and pressed it. The door swished open and he pulled himself upwards and out of the bus.

The gathering crowd watched as a man in

a bright yellow dress hauled himself out of the bus and stood, observing the scene. The emergency services were at the far end, a dozen police cars and ambulances with blue lights flashing. The professor's bus was at the near end, accompanied by more flashing lights. The TV crew managed a close-up of Smith's dazed face, the wind from the helicopter blades making his hair as wild as his expression.

'There's no escape,' said the professor, getting things wrong again.

The TV audience watched as the man walked to the middle of the fallen bus and jumped through the Tower Bridge gap. He plunged downwards, his dress billowing up around him.

'White boxers with red hearts,' noted the news reporter. 'Never a good look.'

Necks craned and breath was held as onlookers strained to see what was happening. The man hit the water with a solid splash, his dress floating at first but then becoming very heavy in the water.

Lara hated to see baddies get away. She did

some quick calculations in her head. *Thirty-metre jump*, she thought. *Into water. I'm a strong swimmer and my fur will keep me warm for a bit longer. The Thames is dangerous but there are plenty of boats if I get into trouble . . .*'Pups, stay here,' she woofed, sprinting towards the middle of the bridge.

The TV news crew zoomed in on the action as a dog took a flying leap towards the water.

Mum regained consciousness for a second time. 'Is it all just a bad dream?' she croaked. 'The bus and everything?'

'Everything's going to be OK,' said Dad as all eyes went back to the TV newsflash. Mum looked dazed as she watched their pet dog execute the perfect dive off Tower Bridge, entering the river with hardly a splash.

'You see,' soothed Dad. 'What did I tell you? Everything is going to be just fine.'

13. Loyal Subjects

The whole family had been invited. Ollie could hardly contain his excitement. '*The Royal Variety Performance*,' he beamed. 'I'll get to meet some celebrities. Is the Queen a celebrity, Dad?' he asked.

Dad smoothed his youngest son's hair. 'The biggest celeb in the world, Ollie,' he confirmed.

The family lined up, hair brushed and nails cleaned. The dogs had been to Pampered Pooches for a makeover. Lara had been blow-dried, Star had had her nails painted and Spud had had his fur trimmed. The professor had a new bow tie, chosen to match his sandals and socks. He looked at the line-up and beamed. 'Perfect,' he grinned. 'Her Majesty will be so proud to meet you.'

As they waited excitedly, the Queen made her way along the line, stopping and shaking hands as she went. A huge royal smile lit up her face as she approached the Cook family. She shook everyone by the hand and the children bowed and curtsied like they'd practised.

'Congratulations,' smiled the Queen. 'Especially to you,' she said, turning her attention to Lara. 'Very heroic. One saw you on the news. One was very impressed with your

bravery. Not only did you manage to capture the baddies,' she praised, turning to the pups, 'but you also stopped them getting away with all the viewers' money.' She left a pause before revealing, 'One of those pounds was mine.' Sophie raised her eyebrows in surprise and the Queen smiled warmly at her. 'Even the Queen votes on *Have You Got Talent?*,' she said.

'One is pretty cool about it,' chirped Ollie, trying out the royal way of speaking. 'It's all in a day's work for one's spy dog and her family.'

The Queen smiled at Ollie. 'What happened to the criminals, young fellow?'

'One was stuck on the toilet,' giggled Ollie.

'Literally,' added Sophie.

Ollie carried on, happy to talk to the Queen. 'The fire brigade had to cut him free. In fact, the professor's ultraglue was so strong that they couldn't actually get the seat off his bottom, so they removed the seat from the toilet. He still has it attached until scientists can work out a formula to remove the glue.'

'It's kind of a cool idea,' added Sophie. 'He now has a toilet seat with him wherever he goes. He's a Portaloo.'

The Queen's eyes sparkled. She loved being head of the country and ruling over her loyal subjects. But those who weren't so loyal deserved to be caught. 'And what about the other villain who jumped into my river?' she enquired.

Ben took over at this point. 'Good news, Your Majesty,' he smiled, puffing out his chest. 'It seems that Darren Smith will be seeing some real judges very soon.'

The Queen returned his smile with interest. 'And your dog?' she asked, nodding towards Lara. 'Your heroic dog that dived in after him? How did she do it?'

'It turned into a rescue mission, ma'am,' explained Ben. 'The man was wearing a huge dress. So when he hit the water he started to sink. Our spy dog here,' he continued as Lara's tail began to wag proudly, 'dragged the man to shore. She basically saved his life. I mean we all helped out in some way. The pups discovered the baddies. Professor Cortex drove the bus. It was a team effort, but it was Lara who did the most important bit.'

I couldn't have done it without you all, agreed

Lara, looking around at her pups, the professor and the children. *But I'm glad Darren Smith and his nephew will have to pay for their crimes, instead of making money from them.*

The Queen shook Lara by the paw. There was a twinkle in her eye. 'Do you know what?' she said to her lady-in-waiting. 'This spy dog's got talent.'

FOR YOUR EYES ONLY – TOP SECRET

MY PET'S GOT TALENT COMPETITION!

CODENAME: TALENTED PETS

Send your entries to:
'Talented Pets'
Puffin
80 Strand
London
WC2R 0RL
By 29th April 2011

Lara is on the hunt for the nation's most talented pets...

Can your goldfish sing opera? Maybe your cat is a computer-game champion. Or is your guinea pig a super-genius?!

Your mission is: send us a poster of your pet showing their talent. Make sure you use lots of **colour**, **imagination** and **creative genius** to prove that YOUR pet is the most talented in the country.

The winning entry will get:
- A Nintendo 3DS, PLUS a game
- featured on www.spydog451.co.uk
- all the Spy Dog and Spy Pup books signed by Andrew Cope and Lara. Wowee!

Five runners-up will get a signed copy of **Spy Pups: Danger Island**.

SPY PUPS: DANGER ISLAND OUT MARCH 2011

Terms and Conditions:

1. No purchase necessary to enter the competition. 2. This competition is open to UK and Ireland residents aged 5 years and over, with the exception of employees of the Promoter, their families, agents and anyone else connected with this promotion. Entries from those age 13 or under must be accompanied by written permission from a parent/guardian or with their written consent. 3. Entries must be received by midnight on 29 April 2011. 4. The Promoter accepts no responsibility for any entries that are incomplete, illegible, corrupted or fail to reach the Promoter by the relevant closing date for any reason. Proof of posting or sending is not proof of receipt. Entries via agents or third parties are invalid. Entries become the property of the Promoter and are not returned. 5. Only one entry per person. No entrant may win more than one prize. 6. To enter, design a poster showing your pet's talent. Then send your entry along with personal details, including name, age, address, phone number, email address and proof of parent/guardian permission to: 'Talented Pets', Puffin, 80 Strand, London, WC2R 0RL. 7. All correctly completed entries will be forwarded to a judging panel made up of Andrew Cope and the Puffin Marketing and Editorial teams. The winner will be the entry that in the opinion of the judges is most colourful, imaginative and creative. 8. The prize for the winner is a Nintendo 3DS (in black), a Nintendo 3DS game (game to be confirmed), and a copy of each of the following books: 'Spy Dog', 'Spy Dog 2', 'Spy Dog Unleashed!', 'Spy Dog Superbrain', 'Spy Dog Rocket Rider', 'Spy Dog Secret Santa', 'Spy Pups Treasure Quest', 'Spy Pups Prison Break', 'Spy Pups Circus Act', and 'Spy Pups Danger Island' all signed by Andrew Cope and with a paw print from Lara. The winning entry will also be featured on www.spydog451.co.uk. Five runners up will win a copy of 'Spy Pups Danger Island' signed by Andrew Cope and with a paw print from Lara. There is no cash alternative available. 9. Prizes are subject to availability. In the event of unforeseen circumstances, the Promoter reserves the right (a) to substitute alternative prizes of equivalent or greater value and (b) in exceptional circumstances to amend or foreclose the promotion without notice. No correspondence will be entered into. 10. The winner will be notified via email or post by 31 May 2011. The winner must claim their prize within 14 working days of the Promoter sending notification. If the prize is unclaimed after this time, it will lapse and the Promoter reserves the right to offer the unclaimed prize to a substitute winner selected in accordance with these rules. 11. To obtain details of the winners please email puffin@penguin.co.uk stating the name of the promotion in the subject heading 4 weeks after the closing date. 12. The Promoter will use any data submitted by entrants only for the purposes of running the prize draw, unless otherwise stated in the entry details. By entering this prize draw, all entrants consent to the use of their personal data by the Promoter for the purposes of the administration of this prize draw and any other purposes to which the entrant has consented. 13. The winners agree to take part in reasonable post-event publicity and to the use of their names and photographs in such publicity. 14. By entering the competition each entrant agrees to be bound by these terms and conditions. 15. The Promoters are Penguin Books Limited, 80 Strand, London, WC2R 0RL.

 Visit the **OFFICIAL** Spy Dog website at **www.spydog451.co.uk**